Dad's

Written by Jack Gabolinscy
Illustrated by Astrid Matijasevic

Rigby

My brother and I went to Dad's place last weekend. Dad met us at the bus stop.

Troy looked at Dad. "It's going to rain tomorrow," he said. "There are black clouds. We won't be able to go fishing."

"It won't rain," said Dad. "I called the weather center and asked for a sunny day. They always give me what I want. See how lucky you are to have a famous father!"

2

The next morning, it was raining cats and dogs. Troy and I were sad. Dad was sad, too. He loved fishing.

"Last time I went fishing," he said, "I caught a record-breaking sardine."(Dad always jokes when he is sad.)

"No worries," he said. "I will cook us a fantastic dinner. I will cook us the biggest and best pasta in the world."

5

In the afternoon we went to the mall. We got the ingredients for Dad's pasta.

When we got home, Dad put on a pink plastic apron and a white hat. "Now I will cook the best dinner of the year," he said in a funny voice.

7

Dad cut the vegetables up. He put them in little heaps around the table. He opened the pasta and tomato paste. He crushed the garlic. He lined up the herbs.

The food smelled wonderful!

Troy and I hung around. We took little tastes when Dad wasn't looking.

But he caught us. "Out! Out! Out!" he roared in his funny voice.

And he chased us out of the kitchen.

9

Sometimes I think that my dad has lost his marbles.

He banged around in the kitchen and sang songs to himself for two hours.

He talked to himself in a funny voice.

Then there was

silence.

The silence went on and on and on.

At last . . .

"Connie!" yelled Dad from the kitchen. "Come here a minute!"

I went into the kitchen.

"Look at this pasta!" he said. He pointed to the pot on the stove.

The pasta was bubbling all over the stove.

"Why is it doing that?" asked Dad.

As we watched, the bubbles grew **bigger** and **bigger**.

They gurgled faster and thicker.

A pretty blue bubble  leaped from the pasta and  floated across the kitchen.

"I know what it is," said Troy. "It's a Blue Bubble Pasta."

"Where do you keep the cooking oil?" I asked Dad.

15

Dad showed me the oil in the cabinet. It was in a yellow plastic bottle with a handle. Next to the oil was another yellow plastic bottle with a handle.

Dishwashing liquid!

On the stove, the pasta bubbled blue and yellow and red. It was like a magic volcano.

Troy and I laughed and laughed.

Dad laughed with us. We were still laughing as we got on the bus to go home.

17

Recounts

Recounts tell about something that has happened.

A recount tells the reader

- what happened

- to whom

- where it happened

- when it happened

A recount has events in sequence . . .

. . . and a conclusion

Guide Notes

> **Title: Dad's Pasta**
> **Stage:** Fluency
>
> **Text Form:** Recount
> **Approach:** Guided Reading
> **Processes:** Thinking Critically, Exploring Language, Processing Information
> **Written and Visual Focus**: Recount Structure, Text Highlights, Speech Bubbles

THINKING CRITICALLY
(sample questions)
- What sort of a person do you think Dad was? How can you tell?
- What do you think Connie meant when she said Dad had lost his marbles?
- Why do you think Dad liked to dress up and talk in a funny voice when he was cooking?
- How do you think Dad could avoid making the same mistake again?

EXPLORING LANGUAGE

Terminology
Spread, author and illustrator credits, ISBN number

Vocabulary
Clarify: ingredients, fantastic, record-breaking
Nouns: house, morning, pasta, apron, dinner
Verbs: cook, cut, chase
Singular/plural: pasta, marble/marbles, recipe/recipes

Print Conventions
Apostrophes – possessives (Dad's pasta, Dad's place), contraction (won't)
Parenthesis: (Dad always jokes when he is sad.)

Phonological Patterns
Focus on short and long vowel **o** (going, jokes, opened, stop, dogs, pot)
Discuss root words – worries, biggest, bubbling
Look at suffix **er** (thicker), **ful** (wonderful)